T3-ALK-665

Very carefully Gregory began to paint one side of the house. He mixed the colors as he went. He gave the boys white clothes. He gave the girls colored dresses—blue, green, and pink.

Ivy helped with the faces. Richard painted in grass and sky.

When they had finished, Uncle Pancho came out to look.

"There I am," he said. "With all my brothers and sisters."

"Do you like it?" asked Ivy.

"I can paint over it," said Gregory.

"Paint over it? No, no, no!" cried the old man. "You must paint more!"

The Paint Brush Kid

The Paint Brush Kid

By

CLYDE ROBERT BULLA

Illustrated by

ELLEN BEIER

A STEPPING STONE BOOK™

Random House  New York

 Published in the United States of America by Random House, Inc., New York, and simultaneously in Canada by Random House of Canada Limited, Toronto.

www.randomhouse.com/kids

Library of Congress Cataloging-in-Publication Data
Bulla, Clyde Robert. The Paint Brush Kid / by Clyde Robert Bulla.
p. cm. "A Stepping Stone book." Summary: Nine-year-old Gregory paints pictures representing the life of the Mexican American old man known as Uncle Pancho and attempts to save him from losing his house.
ISBN 0-679-89282-6 (trade) — ISBN 0-679-99282-0 (lib. bdg.)
[1. Artists—Fiction. 2. Mexican Americans—Fiction.] I. Title.
PZ7.B912Pai 1999 [Fic]—dc21 97-51153

Printed in the United States of America 10 9 8 7 6 5 4 3 2

With thanks to my friends
Phil Sadler, Aileen Helmick, and Ophelia Gilbert
for their years of bringing children and books together

SAM'S GARAGE
HOUSE
PAINTING

Contents

1
Vacation

Gregory was having breakfast with his uncle Max. One piece of toast was left on the table. They were both looking at it.

"Do you want that?" asked Uncle Max.

"You take it," said Gregory.

Uncle Max took it. He crunched into it with his big teeth. "You must be happy," he said.

"Why?" asked Gregory.

"It's vacation," said Uncle Max. "You don't have to go to school today."

"I like school."

"You didn't like it when you first came here."

"I was new. I didn't know anyone."

"But now you're famous. You're the famous Chalk Box Kid." Uncle Max was making a joke. Most of his jokes weren't very funny.

Gregory didn't think he was going to like summer vacation. Mother and Daddy would be at work every day, while he stayed home with his uncle.

Uncle Max didn't have a job. Most of the time he watched television or sang and played his guitar.

"What are you going to do this summer?" Uncle Max asked.

"I don't know," said Gregory. "What are *you* going to do?"

"I guess I'll have to baby-sit you."

Gregory frowned. "I don't need a baby-sitter. I'm going on ten years old."

"That doesn't make you grown-up."

Gregory wanted to say, You're twenty, and you're not grown-up either. But he didn't say it. It would only make trouble.

"May I be excused?" he asked.

He went to look out the window. The street was quiet. It was a street where stores and small factories and people's houses were all mixed together.

A girl was coming up the street. She was walking fast, almost running.

It looked like Ivy. Gregory hoped it was. They had been friends at Dover Street School. She was the best artist in school, although she kept telling him, "No, *you* are the best."

The girl came nearer. She was small, with long black hair. It *was* Ivy.

She had her hand up to knock when he opened the door. She was out of breath. "Is my little brother here?" she asked in her soft, whispering voice.

"No," said Gregory.

"I thought he might be out back," Ivy said.

"Out back" meant the burned building behind the house. Once it had been a chalk factory. Now only three walls were left. When Gregory was cleaning it up, he had found boxes of white chalk. He had drawn a chalk garden on the walls.

"Richard likes your garden," Ivy said. "I thought maybe he came to see it."

They went out back. Gregory opened the gate in the wall. They went into the old building and found themselves standing in the middle of Gregory's garden.

Richard was not there.

"He doesn't mean to run away," said Ivy. "He just gets started and forgets to stop."

They went back to the house. Gregory called in to Uncle Max, "We're going out to find Richard."

Uncle Max said something. Gregory wasn't sure what it was. The television was on.

He and Ivy went down the street. They stopped at Ray's Market and Bob's Barbershop and Sam's Garage. Richard had not been to any of those places.

They came to a house with a sign in front that said: JOHN BRIMM, HOUSE PAINTING. That was where Ivy lived. Her father painted houses.

Her mother stood in the doorway. She was small and round, with long black hair like Ivy's.

"Hello, Mrs. Brimm," said Gregory.

"Hello, Gregory," she said. "Have you seen our boy?"

Gregory shook his head. "No, but we'll keep looking."

He and Ivy continued down the street. They came to Uncle Pancho's.

Everyone called the old man Uncle Pancho, although Ivy said he wasn't really anyone's uncle. He lived alone in the last house on the street.

Gregory knocked at the door. The old man came around the corner of the house. His face was wrinkled and brown. He had bright brown eyes.

"So! You are here to see me," he said. "Come. We will sit together."

He led them into the backyard. And there, in a big chair under an orange tree, sat Richard.

2
Uncle Pancho

"Uncle Pancho knows stories!" said the little boy.

"Why didn't you tell us where you were going?" asked Ivy.

"I didn't know till I got here," he said.

"You have to come home," she said.

"No," said Richard.

"Yes," said Ivy. "We've all been looking

for you."

Uncle Pancho put his hand on the little boy's head. "Go to your mother and father. Tell them you are not lost. Then you can come back."

Slowly Richard got out of the big chair. He waved to Uncle Pancho. Then he went with Gregory and Ivy.

Mr. Brimm was in his truck, out in front of the Brimms' house. He jumped down and picked Richard up. "Where have you been, you little peanut? I was just coming to look for you."

Mrs. Brimm came running out of the house. "You said you wouldn't run away anymore. What are we going to do with you!"

"I didn't run away," said Richard. "There was this cat, and he wouldn't let me catch him. I ran after him. Then I

didn't see him, and I was at Uncle Pancho's, and he told me to come in."

"We thought you were lost," said his father.

"I wasn't lost," said Richard. "I knew where I was."

"But *we* didn't know," said his mother. "You must never go away again without telling us."

They sat on the porch.

"Uncle Pancho must have thought you were lost," said Mrs. Brimm. "He was taking care of you."

"He is a very good man," said Ivy. "Remember when Grandma was sick and you had to stay with her? Uncle Pancho took care of Richard and me. He gave us bread and milk."

"I remember," said Mrs. Brimm. "He helps everybody, but does anybody ever help him?"

"I am going to paint his house," said Mr. Brimm.

"When?" asked his wife.

"When I find time. I am always so busy." Mr. Brimm looked at his watch. "I have to go to work now."

He drove away in his truck.

"Uncle Pancho gave me an orange," said Richard. "I want to go back and get it. Maybe he will tell me another story."

"I'll let you go if your sister goes with you," said Mrs. Brimm. Then she went inside and brought out a loaf of bread. "I just baked this. Take it to Uncle Pancho."

Ivy and Richard went back to Uncle Pancho's. Gregory went with them. Richard found his orange under the big chair. "Tell another story," he said.

"Do you know a place called Mexico?"

the old man began.

"I know *about* it," answered Ivy. "But I've never been there."

"It is where I was born," Uncle Pancho continued. "We had good times there, my brothers and sisters and I. Three sisters, two brothers." He told how they took the goats to pasture. One of the goats was his. He had a pet rooster, too.

Uncle Pancho told about a bridge high over a river. It was a swinging bridge made of rope and vines. "We played on that bridge," he said in a dreamy voice.

He told about a big house where a beautiful lady lived. "She was a great singer. She sang all over the world, and at last she came home. Once she sang just for me—like an angel."

He stopped. His eyes had a faraway look. He seemed to have forgotten that anyone else was there.

"Let's go," whispered Ivy.

She and Richard and Gregory slipped

away.

"Now I know what I want to do on vacation," said Gregory.

"What?" asked Ivy.

"Paint Uncle Pancho's house."

"My father has lots of paint," she said. "He might let us have some, and we could paint together."

"I can paint, too." Richard picked up a stick and pretended it was a paint brush. He swung it back and forth. "Look at me," he cried. "I'm painting!"

3
A New Idea

The next morning Ivy came to see Gregory.

"My father wants to talk to you," she said.

Gregory asked his uncle, "May I go with Ivy?"

Uncle Max was making up a song. He would sing a few words, then go *plink,*

plink on his guitar. "Yes, go, and don't bother me," he said.

Gregory went home with Ivy. Her father was in the garage, among buckets of paint. Richard was there, too.

"So you want to paint Uncle Pancho's house," Mr. Brimm said.

"Yes," said Gregory.

"Do you know how much work that would be?" asked Mr. Brimm. "It wouldn't be like making chalk pictures on a wall."

"I never painted a house," said Gregory, "but I think I could if I had some paint and a brush."

"I could help," said Ivy.

"So could I," Richard said.

"It is not so easy," said Mr. Brimm, "but if you want to, you can try."

He took a little piece of wood and dipped it into a bucket of yellow paint.

"Take this to Uncle Pancho. Ask him if he likes the color."

Gregory and Ivy and Richard found Uncle Pancho out in his yard.

"We're going to paint your house," said Richard.

Gregory showed Uncle Pancho the piece of wood with the paint on it. "Do you like this color?"

The old man held the piece of wood against the house. He nodded. "Yes, yes. It is not too light, not too dark. It is a good yellow."

"My father has lots of it," Ivy told him.

Uncle Pancho looked at them. "Why do you want to paint my house?"

"Because it needs it," said Richard.

"Because our father is always too busy," said Ivy.

"Because we'd like to," said Gregory.

The old man looked a little sad. "I should be painting my own house, but I am not young anymore. It is hard for me to bend down and reach up."

"We can do it," said Gregory. "We can scrape off the old paint, too."

They sat in the backyard and talked about the house.

"I built it with my own hands," Uncle Pancho told them. "That was long ago. Last year I had a scare. Some men said I must give up my house. They were from the government. They said a freeway would come through here. They said it would come across the end of the street and through my house."

"It won't, will it?" asked Ivy.

"I waited and I worried. I could not sleep at night," said Uncle Pancho. "But it was all a mistake. I talked to Bob the barber. He knows about these things. He says the freeway will not come through here. He says not to worry. So I do not worry."

Richard was up on the table.

"What are you doing? You will fall," said the old man.

Richard pointed up to the tree. "I want that big orange. Then I want you to tell another story."

Uncle Pancho picked the orange for him. "Now I'll tell you a story. It is a true story. It is about a boy like you."

"What is his name?" asked Richard.

"José," answered the old man. "His name is José. All the time he wanted to be with me. He rode on my back. I pulled him in a cart. Can you guess who he was?"

Richard shook his head.

"He was my son," said Uncle Pancho.

Ivy looked up in surprise. "I never knew you had a son."

"Where is he?" asked Richard.

"His mother took him away," said Uncle Pancho. "She was tired of staying with me and being poor. One day I came home from work, and she and José were gone. I followed them. I wanted my son. Sometimes I was close to them. Then I lost them. Someone said they had gone north, so I came here."

"Did you find them?" asked Richard.

"I saw this big city, and I did not look anymore. In this city, who could find anyone? I know now that I will never find my son. And that is my sad story."

"It wasn't all sad," said Richard. "I liked the part about your brothers and sisters."

"And the story isn't over," said Ivy. "Maybe you *will* find José."

"No, no," said Uncle Pancho. "There is no way."

Gregory had been listening. An idea was coming to him. "When we paint your house," he said, "how would you feel if we

painted pictures?"

The old man looked puzzled. "Pictures?"

"Pictures on your house. Pictures of your life!" Gregory was excited. "There could be one over the door and one on each side of it. There could be a big one across the back and a little one between the windows."

"Pictures?" the old man said again. Suddenly he looked angry. "You want to make my house something for people to look at and laugh at?"

"No!" said Gregory.

"Forget your pictures. Forget your paint. My house is nothing for you to have fun with!"

The old man was shaking with anger. He got up and went into the house. The door banged shut behind him.

4
At Mr. Hiller's

Gregory walked home with Ivy and Richard. They were quiet.

"Aren't we going to paint Uncle Pancho's house?" asked Richard as they stopped at the gate to his house.

Ivy didn't answer.

"I wouldn't have made pictures if he didn't wanted me to," said Gregory.

He started to go. Ivy went with him a little way. She said, "It's all right."

But it was not all right. Gregory kept remembering how angry Uncle Pancho had been.

"What's the matter with you?" asked Uncle Max. "Today you look like the Bad News Kid."

Gregory didn't feel like talking. He went out back and sat in the burned building. He looked at his chalk garden.

He liked to draw and paint on paper, but a piece of paper never seemed big enough. What he really liked was making pictures on walls. Drawing his chalk garden was the best time he had ever had.

But sometimes Gregory had wished for color in his garden. He had wished he could *paint* on a wall, and he thought about the pictures he could have painted on Uncle Pancho's house.

The day went by very slowly.

Mother and Daddy came home from work. Mother was a cook in a restaurant. Daddy was a guard in a bank.

Daddy told Gregory, "Someone asked about you in the bank today."

"About me?" asked Gregory.

"Yes. Mr. Hiller."

Mr. Hiller had a nursery three blocks away. It was a plant nursery where he sold plants and seeds.

He had given Gregory the idea for the chalk garden. He had come to Gregory's school and talked about gardens. He had brought plants and seeds for the boys and girls.

Gregory had had no place to plant a garden. There was concrete all around his house and the burned-out chalk factory in back, so he had made his garden in white chalk on the walls of the burned building.

Mr. Hiller had heard about the garden. He had come over and taken pictures of it.

"He wanted to know if you were making any more gardens," said Daddy.

"No," said Gregory. "I don't have any

more walls."

"What did you do all day?" asked Mother.

"All he did was mope," said Uncle Max.

"I didn't mope," said Gregory.

"Is something wrong?" asked Mother.

Gregory wanted to tell her and Daddy what had happened, but not in front of his uncle. Uncle Max would only laugh and make jokes.

"I'm all *right,*" he said.

They had dinner. Gregory kept thinking about Mr. Hiller. Mr. Hiller was someone he could talk to.

"May I be excused?" he asked. "I want to go to the nursery."

"What for?" asked Mother.

"Well...Mr. Hiller asked about me."

"It's late," said Mother. "The nursery will be closed."

"He'll be there," said Gregory. "He lives in the back."

"Go ahead," said Daddy, "but be home before dark."

Gregory walked the three blocks to Mr. Hiller's nursery. It was closed, but Mr. Hiller was there, watering plants.

He saw Gregory through the glass door and let him in.

The air was damp inside the nursery. There were plants everywhere. Some of them had strange flowers that didn't look real.

"Sit down," said Mr. Hiller. "What's on your mind?"

"Do you know Uncle Pancho?" asked Gregory.

"We're old friends," said Mr. Hiller.

"I don't know him very well, and I must have said the wrong thing to him.

We were going to paint his house—Ivy, Richard, and I, and I had this idea. I said I'd like to paint pictures on his house."

"Pictures? On his house?"

"Yes. And all at once he changed. He

wasn't friendly anymore. He thought I wanted to make his house look funny."

Mr. Hiller looked thoughtful. "There aren't many houses with pictures painted on them, are there?"

"But I wouldn't have made his house look funny. He might have liked it. He told us about his life, and I wanted to make pictures of it."

"He's a good man," Mr. Hiller said. "But sometimes he loses his temper. I don't think he understood what you wanted to do."

"No, I don't think he did." Gregory looked out. It was getting dark. "I have to go."

"I could talk to him," said Mr. Hiller.

"About the pictures?"

"Yes."

"He probably doesn't want to talk about them."

"I could tell him what you told me. It couldn't do any harm, could it?"

"No," said Gregory. And as he started home, he began to feel better.

5
A Visitor

The next morning Gregory was out in his garden. He liked to see it at different times of the day. Now the white chalk was bright. It seemed to stand out from the walls. In the afternoon it would have a softer look.

He took a piece of chalk and drew a few more leaves on a tree. Then he rubbed them out. The tree had enough leaves. There wasn't much more he could do to his garden.

He heard footsteps. There was a man at the gate—a man in a big hat.

It was Uncle Pancho!

Gregory opened the gate.

"You want me to come in?" asked the old man.

"Yes!" said Gregory.

"After what I said yesterday? I said things that were not so good."

"It doesn't matter," said Gregory.

"I knew there was an artist boy on this street, but I did not know it was you. Joe Hiller came and told me. Now I know you are the Chalk Box Kid."

Gregory felt a little foolish. "They call me that sometimes."

"I thought you wanted to make pic-

tures on my house so people would laugh. I did not know—" Uncle Pancho had come into the old building. He was looking at the garden on the walls—the rows of vegetables and flowers, the trees, and the fountain.

"This is *good,*" he said. "Yesterday I did not know. Now you may not want to paint my house."

"I was thinking—" began Gregory.

"What were you thinking, my chicken?"

"First we could paint your house with the yellow paint. Then I could paint one picture. If you didn't like it, I could paint over it."

"Yes." The old man nodded. "Let us see."

~

They started work that afternoon—Gregory, Ivy, and Richard. They scraped the old paint off Uncle Pancho's house. Gregory and Ivy did most of the scraping. Richard swept up the old paint and put it into buckets.

Mr. Brimm brought over the yellow paint. He brought some brushes and a ladder.

"It won't be easy," he told them.

"This is fun," Richard said, painting with his own little brush. But soon he was tired. He kept stopping to drink the lemonade his mother had brought.

Gregory and Ivy grew tired, too. The house was bigger than they had thought.

It took them a week to finish.

"What a nice yellow house!" said Uncle Pancho.

"Maybe you won't want any pictures on it," said Gregory.

"Wait till it is dry," said the old man. "Then we will see."

Gregory and Ivy talked about the pictures.

"One could be of Uncle Pancho when he was a boy," said Gregory, "with his brothers and sisters."

"And the swinging bridge over the river," said Ivy. "If he does want pictures on his house, I think they should be yours. Big pictures are what you like to make. All mine are small."

"We could still work together," Gregory told her. "There are little things in big pictures."

"You mean like houses or trees or people a long way off?" she asked.

"Yes," he said. "And you could do faces. Your faces are better than mine."

"No, yours are better. But I'll do some if you want me to."

They looked for paint in the colors they would need. Mr. Brimm had some colors he used to mix his paints. Mr. Hiller brought Gregory four big tubes of white, red, blue, and yellow.

"You can mix them," he said, "and

make any color you want."

"Do you like your house better the way it is?" Gregory asked Uncle Pancho.

"The yellow house is nice," said the old man, "but paint a picture, and we will see."

Gregory started the first picture. On one side of the house he made outlines in chalk. He made outlines of the boy Pancho and his two brothers and three sisters. They were all in a row. Very carefully he began to paint. He used the small brushes Mr. Hiller had brought. He mixed the colors as he went. He gave the boys white clothes. He gave the girls colored dresses—blue, green, and pink.

Ivy helped with the faces. Some were happy. Some were serious. No two were alike, yet they all looked like brothers and

sisters.

Richard painted in grass and sky.

They asked Uncle Pancho not to look until they had finished.

People came by to watch them. Some of them shook their heads. A man said, "You kids are making a mess of that house."

"Do you think we are?" Ivy asked Gregory.

"No," he said.

One day Uncle Pancho came out to look.

"There I am," he said. "With all my brothers and sisters."

"Do you like it?" asked Ivy.

"I can paint over it," said Gregory.

"Paint over it? No, no, no!" cried the old man. "You must paint more!"

6

The Man from the State

For days and weeks the work went on. Gregory did most of the painting, but Ivy was there to help. Sometimes Richard painted a little grass or a piece of sky.

When they ran out of paint, Mr. Hiller brought more.

Every day people came to watch. At first Gregory had felt shy, but after a while he forgot they were there. He forgot about everything but the pictures.

One day the front of the house was finished. It was covered with two big pictures and a smaller one.

Uncle Pancho pointed to the picture of the swinging bridge. "I played there when I was a boy. How did you know how it looked?"

"You told me," answered Gregory.

He painted other things from the old man's stories. The mountains of Mexico. The house where the lady singer had lived. The little roads.

The last picture was nearly finished.

"What is this?" asked Uncle Pancho.

"A picture of you," said Gregory.

"I can see that. But the other man—who is he?"

"That was going to be a surprise," said Gregory. "I'll paint over it if you don't like it. That is your son."

"But my son was a little boy."

"He is grown-up now. That is how he looks. That is how I think he looks."

"You paint us here in my yard—by my orange tree. You think I will still find him?"

"Maybe. Maybe you will find each

other."

Uncle Pancho looked at the picture for a long time. "What a good friend you are! I give up, but you do not give up. And it may be I was wrong to give up. Maybe it will be just as you are painting it here, and I will find José again."

They worked on the last picture—Gregory, Ivy, and Richard. A crowd was there to watch. One man spoke to Gregory. He was someone Gregory had never seen before. He wore a dark blue suit and a tie. "That's nice," he said. "But why are you going to all that trouble?"

"It's no trouble," said Gregory.

"It's for Uncle Pancho," Ivy added.

"Don't you know this house has to go?" asked the man.

Someone in the crowd spoke to him. "You're from the state, aren't you?"

"Yes, I am," answered the man. "The freeway is going across this end of the street. We told the man who lives here."

"The freeway people changed their minds," said Gregory.

"They never changed their minds," said the man. "Your Uncle Pancho heard just what he wanted to hear. We're going to have to take his house."

"You mean tear it down?" asked Gregory.

"That's what I mean," the man said. Then he went away.

Gregory and Ivy had stopped painting. Richard came up to them. "What did you stop for?"

The people on the sidewalk were talking. Someone said, "Too bad." Someone

else said, "I'm sorry." They began to leave.

Gregory, Ivy, and Richard went into the backyard. Uncle Pancho came out. "Why are they going away?" he asked.

"The freeway is coming through," whispered Ivy.

"No, no!" said the old man.

"He said they told you," said Gregory.

"That was long ago. The freeway will *not* go through."

"The man just told us," said Gregory. "The house will have to go."

"It will not!" The old man was shouting. "Bob the barber says it will not!"

Ivy and Gregory looked at each other. "Maybe the barber doesn't know," she whispered.

Uncle Pancho started to speak. He stopped. Suddenly he looked very old and very tired. He turned and went slowly into the house.

Ivy took Richard's hand. "We're going home."

They waited a few moments for Gregory. Then they went away without him.

Gregory was looking at the last picture. It was finished except for the shadows of the two men.

I have to finish, he thought. *I have to know how it looks. Even if they tear it down tomorrow, I have to finish.*

He picked up a paint brush and went back to painting. He knew it was his best picture ever.

7
The Television Show

Before Gregory finished, he had a visitor. Someone came into the yard and called his name.

He was up on the ladder. He looked down. A woman was there. It was the woman who had been his art teacher at school.

"Miss Cartright!" he said.

"I heard you had gone on to bigger things," she said, "and I came to see. Gregory, this is amazing!"

He came down the ladder.

"What gave you such an idea?" she asked.

"The stories Uncle Pancho told," answered Gregory. "They were about his life. Ivy and I turned them into pictures. But they won't be here much longer."

"And why not?" asked Miss Cartright.

"The freeway is coming through. We just found out. The house has to go."

"We'll see about that," said Miss Cartright.

~

Miss Cartright came to Gregory's house that evening. Her cheeks were pink. She looked excited. "I have a plan," she said.

Her plan was to put Uncle Pancho's house on television. "And we'll write letters and put up signs that say, 'Save the Picture House.'"

"People won't know what that means," said Gregory's father.

"They will when they see it in the newspapers and on television." Miss Cartright was growing more excited. "We'll get the whole city behind us. The freeway will have to go somewhere else."

Television people came to see Uncle Pancho's house. They came to see Gregory and Ivy.

Ivy hid under her bed.

"She won't be on television," said her mother. "She is too shy."

Miss Cartright had a talk with Gregory. "You may be shy, too, but the pictures were your idea. You are the important one. At a time like this you have to be brave."

Gregory went to see Mr. Hiller. "Do I have to be brave?"

"I think you do," said Mr. Hiller, "if you want to save the house."

"Do you think we can save it?"

"I don't know," said Mr. Hiller, "but something good could come out of this. I've been talking with Uncle Pancho. Do you know about his son?"

"Yes. Uncle Pancho doesn't know where he is."

"Stories are coming out in the newspapers about the Picture House," said Mr.

Hiller. "A lot of people will see them. When the story comes out on television, thousands more will know about Uncle Pancho. One of them might be his son. He might see the television show and—"

"They might find each other!" Gregory said.

"It could happen. Let's hope this story goes all over the country. Let's hope José hears about it."

Gregory and Uncle Pancho had their pictures taken for the television show. They were in front of the Picture House. Gregory had a paint brush in his hand. He told how he and Ivy and Richard had tried to paint the story of Uncle Pancho's life. Uncle Pancho told how he had come from Mexico to find his son, José.

"This house I built with my own hands," he said. "Now my son will know where to find me—in the house with the pictures."

The television announcer said, "There is talk that the new freeway will come through and take this house with all its wonderful paintings, but this cannot happen. This house must be kept for everyone to see."

Cameramen were there. They took pictures of every painting.

Uncle Max had written a song about the Picture House. He wanted to sing it on the show, but the television people said there was no place for it.

The show went on the air that night. All the next day the little street was crowded. People had come to see the house. Gregory and Uncle Pancho were

there to talk with them.

Whenever Gregory saw a man with dark hair and brown eyes, he would whisper to Uncle Pancho, "Is that José?"

The old man would whisper back, "When he comes, we will know each other."

Miss Cartright was happy with everything. A few days after the television show, she came to Gregory and said, "I'm on my way to talk with the freeway people. I think I may have good news for you."

Gregory waited. In less than an hour she was back. He was at the door to meet her. One look at her face told him what the news would be.

"They wouldn't change their plans," she said. "The house will have to go. I'm sorry. I worked so hard. We all worked so hard." She began to cry.

Gregory went to the nursery to tell Mr. Hiller.

"We'd better go tell Uncle Pancho," said Mr. Hiller.

He closed the nursery. Then he and Gregory walked over to the Picture House.

Uncle Pancho came to the door with his head bowed. He had already heard the news.

"There were so many people on my side, I thought they would save my house, but it was not to be," he said. "I thought my son would come, but that was not to be. It was all for nothing."

"It was not all for nothing," said Mr. Hiller. "I know someone else who will be your son—if you will have him."

"Who?" asked Uncle Pancho.

"Me," said Mr. Hiller.

8
A Celebration

They sat in the little house. Uncle Pancho and Mr. Hiller talked, and Gregory listened.

Mr. Hiller said, "You know where I live, in back of the nursery. There is room for two houses. We could move your house next to mine. Would you like that?"

"Why do you do these things for me?"

asked the old man.

"I told you," said Mr. Hiller. "I'm going to be your son."

One day men came and lifted the house and set it on wheels. Late at night, when there were only a few cars on the street, the men brought a tractor and moved the house away. Very slowly they pulled it around one corner after another. Then they set it down beside Mr. Hiller's house behind the nursery.

There had been a celebration when the Picture House was shown on television. Now there was another celebration. A crowd gathered around the Picture House. There was food and there was music.

People sang and danced. They began dancing around Uncle Pancho's big hat, and he danced with them. His face was not old and sad now. He looked almost young again.

There was a microphone. Mr. Hiller made a speech.

"When we moved the house, we ran into a telephone pole," he said. "A little paint was knocked off one of the pictures. We called Gregory, and he painted it as good as new. Gregory is the one who had the idea for the Picture House. Now I think we would all like to hear from him."

"No!" said Gregory. "I don't know what

to say."

"Just say what you are thinking," said Mr. Hiller, pulling the microphone down so Gregory could reach it.

The crowd grew quiet. Gregory saw boys and girls from his school. His mother and father were there, and so were Mr. and Mrs. Brimm and Ivy and Richard.

"When vacation started," he began, "I didn't know what I was going to do, but my friends and I found something. Ivy and Richard and I—we worked together and painted Uncle Pancho's house and put pictures on it. It's been a good vacation. I hope all my vacations are as good as this one."

Gregory could not think of anything more to say. People began to shout and clap.

Uncle Max came out of the crowd.

"I'd like to sing the song I wrote," he said.

He had his guitar, and he played and sang:

"This is what somebody dreamed,
This is what somebody did.
So give three cheers for the Picture House
And three for the Paint Brush Kid!"

Gregory listened. He had not known his uncle could sing so well.

About the Author

CLYDE ROBERT BULLA was born on a farm near King City, Missouri. He went to a one-room country school. Reading and writing were his favorite subjects, and by the time he was seven, he knew he wanted to be a writer. After years of writing magazine stories and novels and working on his hometown newspaper, he found that he really wanted to write for children. More than seventy of his books for boys and girls have been published. He lives in Los Angeles and divides his time between writing and traveling.

Gregory's garden grew from
his imagination in

The Chalk Box Kid

At school the girls and boys talked about their gardens.

Miss Perry asked Gregory, "How is your garden?"

"All right," he said. "I have poles with sweet peas on them."

Miss Perry said, "That's nice. What else do you have?"

"Vegetables," he told her. "And I have a path to the pool."

She looked surprised. "Your garden must be big."

"It is," he said.

And he had plans to make it bigger.

He took the ladder out of the garage. He set it up in the garden room. When he was on the ladder, he could reach the top of the walls. Now he could have trees in his garden.

He made a pear tree and a walnut tree. He made vines to hang from the branches. He made birds' nests in the trees…